The author and illustrator developed a wonderful story. This book articulates the relationship between a police officer and his horse and how they are on constant watch to ensure their neighborhood is safe! When the moment strikes, both are ready to spring into action to help a woman in need and catch the thief. The story also demonstrates the positive relationship between the police and the community.

Cynthia McAlister
Chief of Police

**Concerns of Police Survivors**

A portion of the proceeds will go to the police department

To order additional copies of this book, contact:
Xlibris
1-888-795-4274
www.Xlibris.com
Orders@Xlibris.com

In the police stable there is a special horse with a special heart shaped patch of hair on his shoulder. His name is Patches.

Patches the police horse woke up to a sunny morning. As he looked out of his stall window, he was excited to see Officer Mike coming up the walkway to the police stable. He comes every morning to feed Patches and get him ready for their work day.

Officer Mike fed, groomed and rode Patches. They were partners and Patches liked him very much. After morning feed and grooming Patches was saddled up and the two rode their route around the park, sometimes stopping to talk with people. Often, people would ask Officer Mike if they could pet Patches. Of course, the answer was always, "yes." He loved being petted and Officer Mike always enjoyed talking to them.

Most days were spent in this happy routine. Even while Officer Mike talked to people, he was always watching to see if the park looked safe and that no one needed help. While Patches loved his work, sometimes he wished something exciting would happen.

At noon they would stop for lunch. If they were close to the stable, Patches would be ridden there, otherwise they would go back to the horse trailer for their lunch break. Officer Mike would loosen the girth to the saddle, take off Patches' bridle and put a halter on his head. This made it easier for Patches to eat his hay. He was also given a bucket of water, and sometimes a carrot. He loved lunchtime! After taking care him, Officer Mike would have his lunch, too.

When lunch was over, Patches' bridle was put back on his head, his girth was tightened, and off they went on their afternoon patrol, ready to meet people and help anyone in need. Officer Mike enjoyed meeting boys and girls and he often talked to them about the heart shaped patch of hair on Patches' shoulder. Officer Mike patiently answered all their questions about his job and of course, Patches!

Sometimes they would meet other police horses and officers and stand together while the officers discussed their work. The horses could stand and watch people and sometimes take a little afternoon nap if the Officers talked a long time. Often they would finish up their patrol with another horse and officer. Patches always enjoyed the company of other horses!

At the end of their work day they returned to the stable. Officer Mike put patches in his stall and removed his bridle and saddle. Next he would be brushed, or if it had been a hot day, Patches would be given a nice cool bath outside in the stable yard, he loved that!

When brushing or bath time was finished, Patches was given his evening feed and a big bucket of cool, clean water. Officer Mike would always give him a nice pat and say "Good night Patches, you were great today." Then he would open the stall door and let Patches out of the stable so he could spend the evening free to run and graze in his pasture. As he watched Patches trot out of the stable, Officer Mike said "I'll see you in the morning," and he left to go home to his wife and children.

The next morning while Officer Mike and Patches were in the park on their morning patrol, they heard a woman yell, "Stop that man, he stole my purse!" They turned and saw a tall man with a purse tucked under his arm running across the soccer field towards the woods.

In a flash, Patches and Officer Mike were off chasing the man with the stolen purse. He was already half way across the field and Patches knew he'd have to gallop as fast as he could to reach the man before he entered the woods where it would be very difficult to catch him.

As they galloped closer and closer to the man with purse, Officer Mike yelled, "Police Officer, stop," but the man continued to run. Finally, just at the edge of the field, Patches was close enough to run in front of the man and block his way to the woods. Officer Mike told the man to drop the purse and put up his hands. The man did as he was told. Within minutes a police car arrived and they placed the man under arrest and took him to the police station.

Officer Mike told Patches how fast and wonderful he was. Quickly the people in the Park who saw the chase came up to Patches and Officer Mike to tell them how brave they were and thank them for being there to help.

At the end of day, while they were on their ride back to the barn, Officer Mike talked to Patches and told him he was a great horse. He said Patches did a wonderful job chasing down and blocking the man with the stolen purse.

When they reached the stable, everyone came to Patches' stall to congratulate him and Officer Mike on the successful chase and arrest of the man with the purse. It was a very exciting day and Patches was glad they could help the kind lady in the park. Helping people is their job!

That evening, Officer Mike gave Patches extra grain and carrots for his job well done. As the Officer left the stable he gave him a nice pat and said, "Good night Patches. You were a hero today! I'll see you in the morning."

To the men and women who risk their lives every day to protect us, and in honor of those who have lost their lives in the line of duty.

Also written by Claire LaBelle Rolince

Lefty Louie

The Day The Animals Talked

Printed in the United States
by Baker & Taylor Publisher Services